TITCHY WITCH

AND THE STRAY DRAGON

For Cassie
R.I.

For Deli
K.M.

ORCHARD BOOKS
338 Euston Road, London NW1 3BH
Orchard Books Australia
Level 17/207 Kent Street, Sydney, NWS 2000
First published in Great Britain in 2003
First paperback publication in 2004
This edition published in 2015
ISBN 978 1 40833 788 2
Text © Rose Impey 2003 Illustrations © Katharine McEwen 2003
The rights of Rose Impey to be identified as the author and
Katharine McEwen to be identified as the illustrator of this Work
have been asserted by them in accordance with the
Copyright, Designs and Patents Act, 1988.
A CIP catalogue record for this book is available from the British Library
1 3 5 7 9 10 8 6 4 2
Printed in China
Orchard Books is a division of Hachette Children's Books,
an Hachette UK company
www.hachette.co.uk

TITCHY WITCH

AND THE STRAY DRAGON

ROSE IMPEY ★ KATHARINE McEWEN

ORCHARD

Titchy-witch

Victor

Eric

Wendel

Weeny-witch

Witchy-witch

Cat-a-bogus

Titchy-witch *really* wanted a pet.
But Witchy-witch said,
"I'm sorry, my little
charmer."

"There are too many pets in this
house already," said Cat-a-bogus.

Cat-a-bogus wasn't a pet.
He was Witchy-witch's magic
cat and he thought he was
the boss of the house!

Victor wasn't *much* of a pet.
He was too old and sleepy.

And Eric wasn't
at all friendly.

Anyway, Titchy-witch wanted
a pet of her own.
So she tried to magic one.

"Scales, skin, feather, fur.
Hiss, growl, woof, purr.
Don't care what I get.
Just bring me a pet!"

Luckily her spells didn't
last very
long.

One morning, Titchy-witch heard a noise outside.

It was love at first sight.

The baby dragon put his head
in her lap.

"Oh, no," said Cat-a-bogus.
"No, no, no, no, no."

When Mum and Dad came home, they said "no" too.

But he's so cute!

"He won't be cute when he's grown," said Witchy-witch. "He'll roar his head off."
"And breathe fire everywhere," said Wendel.

He'll be a dragon!

They led the baby dragon outside.
"Go and find your mummy."

But the next morning the baby
dragon was still there, looking
up at the door, hopefully.

So they took him to the Dragon
Rescue Centre.

When they saw all the baby
dragons with no homes to go to,
they couldn't bear to leave him.

"You can keep him while he's
a baby," said Mum and Dad,
"but when he's bigger than you...
he has to go!"
"Superdoodle!" squealed
Titchy-witch.

I shall call
him Dido!

Dido slept in a basket by her bed,
or sometimes on the end of it.

Titchy-witch and Dido went
everywhere together.
He even went with her
to school, at least as far
as the gates.

At home the little dragon helped Titchy-witch with her homework.

And sometimes with her spells!

Titchy-witch was very happy, and so was Dido.

But then he started to grow.

Soon he was almost as tall as her.

Titchy-witch decided, if Dido had to go, she would go too.
She decided to fly away.

When everyone was asleep,
Titchy-witch and Dido
crept downstairs.

But the little dragon was so heavy
now, the broomstick
could hardly take off.

It kept crash landing.
In the end they woke
Cat-a-bogus!

"Dido keeps on growing," Titchy-
witch explained, "so we're flying
away." Cat-a-bogus purred,
while he thought about this.

The truth was, Dido was very useful in the kitchen. The cat didn't want to lose his little helper.

The next day Cat-a-bogus helped
Titchy-witch make a special
shrinking spell.

"Teeny, tiny
weeny, wink.
Make this little
dragon shrink!"

Dido shrank until he was
just the right size.
He didn't mind, as long as he could
stay with Titchy-witch.

"Have you noticed Dido never seems to grow?" said Dad. "He must be a special *small* kind of dragon," said Mum.

Titchy-witch gave Dido
a big cuddle.
Oh, yes, he was a *special*
dragon all right.

TITCHY WITCH

BY ROSE IMPEY   ILLUSTRATED BY KATHARINE McEWEN

Enjoy a little more magic with all the Titchy-witch tales:

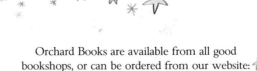

Orchard Books are available from all good
bookshops, or can be ordered from our website:
www.orchardbooks.co.uk
or telephone 01235 827702, or fax 01235 827703.

Prices and availability are subject to change.